THIS WALKER BOOK BELONGS TO:

_____

_____

_____

WALKER BOOKS
AND SUBSIDIARIES
LONDON · BOSTON · SYDNEY · AUCKLAND

For Cheryl

This edition published in Great Britain 2005 by
Walker Books Ltd, 87 Vauxhall Walk, London SE11 5HJ

20 19 18 17 16 15 14 13

© 2004 Mo Willems

First published in the United States by Hyperion Books for Children.
British publication rights arranged with Sheldon Fogelman Agency, Inc.

This book has been handlettered by Mo Willems

Printed in Malaysia   All rights reserved

ISBN 978-1-84428-545-7

British Library Cataloguing in Publication Data:
a catalogue record for this book is available from the British Library

www.walker.co.uk

The Pigeon Finds a Hot Dog!

words and pictures by mo willems

I have a
question.

What do they taste like?

Of course! Enjoy!

Go
on.

T'S IT!

You know, you're pretty clever for a duckling.

WALKER BOOKS is the world's leading
independent publisher of children's books.
Working with the best authors and illustrators
we create books for all ages, from babies
to teenagers – books your child will
grow up with and always remember. So…

FOR THE BEST CHILDREN'S BOOKS,
LOOK FOR THE BEAR